Sorry for ...
Bob McEwen

Casey Joe MacBride's
White River, Vol. I

as told to R. F. McEwen

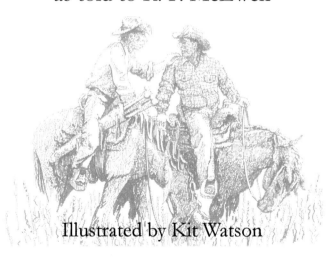

Illustrated by Kit Watson

STEPHEN F. AUSTIN STATE UNIVERSITY PRESS
NACOGDOCHES ★ TEXAS

Cover Illustration by Kit Watson
Book Design by Andrea Laham

Published by Stephen F. Austin State University Press
Box 13007, SFA Station
Nacogdoches, Texas 75962
936-468-1078
http://www.sfasu.edu/sfapress/
sfapress@sfasu.edu

Library of Congress Cataloging-in-Publication Data

McEwen, R. E.
Casey Joe MacBride's White River Vol. 1 /
R. E. McEwen

ISBN 978-1-62288-067-6

1. Native American - Memoir 2. Great Plains Literature   3. Poetry

This work is dedicated to

Velma (Unci) Lame

Chuck Canaday
Eliza Little Spotted Horse
Sampson Bearkiller
Louis Pretty Boy

Richard and Bonnie Swallow, Silas Grant
Pete and Bernice Brown Eyes, Aunty Pearl McClain
Johnny and Beatrice Weasel Bear

Joe Roan Eagle and Morris Yellow Horse, Sr.

"Stacking Rick Wood: Getting On"
published in Nebraska Poets Calendar *Black Star Press*,
2012, Lincoln, Nebraska.

Table of Contents

6   R. F. McEwen

Introduction

Frank Bearkiller was the first one to plant the seed for *White River, Vol. I*, by Casey Joe MacBride, sometime around 1980. We were banging away at a huge block of elm wood we were trying to quarter so we could manage it out of the backyard at 362 Crescent Drive in Lincoln, Nebraska, and into the truck sitting out in the driveway. Greg Wills and Frank and I had teamed up on a huge Siberian Elm for $550.00, and now that we had it on the ground and the brush hauled, we were working on getting the trunk out by dark. Greg and I had taken turns in the top, and Frank worked ground, roping down what the climber cut; the other, either Greg or I, would then drag that section out to the truck and load it. We had a pretty good day. As long as we kept moving, we stayed warm.

It was in the 20s, no doubt about that, and now, closing in on four p.m. and with everything including tools (except a 9 lb beater, three wedges, and an axe) in the truck, we could feel the temperature beginning to drop slowly into the teens. Greg and I each took a turn, but the chunk had a knot in it and we couldn't even get a wedge started. Frank was just returning from the truck.

"I thought you boys would have that quartered by now," he said. "It's going to get dark and cold and scary pretty soon, and we don't want to be anywhere near here when it does." Greg and I were hoping Frank would make short work of stashing the saws in the truck and finding his way back to take over on the chunk. We'd gotten the rest, all straight grain, with no trouble; this one had us licked. And without putting too fine an edge on it, that's saying a lot.

Greg's a bit over six feet tall and weighs in at 180 lbs; he's been a tree man all his life (he was pushing fifty then) and can split wood. I'm about six years senior, and I'd been working tree jobs since I was seventeen years old. I'm about eight inches shorter than Greg and weigh in at about 150. I can split wood, too. But this block had us beat. Usually with a knotty block like this one, you just took the chain to it, but, by that time, Frank had the saws put away. Besides, Greg and I had gotten it into our minds that this was a block that would be split. Of course, if you were in the wood business full-time you'd have a hydraulic wood splitter to make short work of knots. Well, I don't want to write a book about why we didn't have a log splitter.

We were all doing something else full-time then: Greg had found a pretty good inside winter job as a boilermaker, Frank was programming computers, and I was an instructor at the University of Nebraska at Lincoln and doing graduate work. Greg, though, had his own tree business, and I was also working trees at UNL campus and for Twyla Hansen over at Nebraska Wesleyan. Frank had been working wood all his life, too, mostly to keep warm up in Shannon County, South Dakota. We all came together on side jobs, though, on weekends and when any one of us needed extra hands. We were not in the firewood business.

And now here was Frank: about my age but closer to Greg's height and with close to a hundred more pounds. As I write this, Frank has dropped those hundred and a bit more. Back at 362 Crescent Drive, though, he was a lad to be reckoned with; he still is, just minus a pound or two.

"If you give me a bit of room here, I'll show you how River Rats split wood up in White River country," he said as he took the sledge hammer from Greg and a wedge from me. When the head of Frank Bearkiller's hammer hit that wedge, the whole of Crescent Drive shivered its timbers; the block of elm wood shattered; lights went on; the sound of infants rousing early from late-afternoon naps could be heard throughout the neighborhood; police cars cruised the block; the shock waves shriveled conversation for a week. Greg Wills and I were glad Frank was on our side.

"Short work," Frank said and handed the beater back to Greg; the wedge has yet to resurface.

Then, in a blink, we had the wood entrucked, the yard cleaned, the check in hand (Mr. Dannar, our customer, said his head was still quaking from whatever we used to "blow that wood with") and were headed out to the North dump when Frank asked me about Casey Joe MacBride.

"I'm surprised you two never met up," he said; "he went to Chadron State College about the same time you did. And he and his family lived over on Chapin, I think. In fact, his grandfather was pretty good friends with my dad, he and his buddy Carlos. I think they were from up around Kyle, maybe Fast Horse Creek. They were even hauling wood up to Wounded Knee, just like we were. He knew Davey and Don Roy, too. Didn't you ever run into him out at Slim Buttes? At Joe Roan Eagle's?"

Yes, I did remember Casey Joe. He was a History major at Chadron State College while I was there. And yes, I had seen him up at Wounded Knee a time or two. He'd been born in that country, though. I didn't get to the northwestern end of Nebraska and the southwestern end of South Dakota until I was a bit over twenty.

"MacBride wasn't much of a talker then," I said, "or we just didn't have too much to say to each other. He was a year or two ahead of me. Why would you bring him up?"

"Oh, I don't know. He's been teaching History at Clayton for about five years now. I ran into him in Omaha a few months back and he asked about you."

"About me?"

"Wanted to know if you were still writing."

"I am, but what's that to him?"

"He never said."

We dumped our wood without incident that early evening, just before the dump closed. People ask, "Don't you keep the wood and sell it?" Which is a good question. But unless you're in the firewood business full time and have a place to split, stack, and store, it's just more work than you care to deal with.

"Well, didn't you ask?" I was tempted to put to Frank later, at the café. I didn't, though. Frank never was one to go after something that didn't want to be caught. He'd give an ear, open a door, blink an eye; the rest was up to you.

About three years ago, though, during our Christmas break at Chadron State, where I'd been teaching English since 1986, Frank came back to check up on some relatives of his.

Over dinner, Casey Joe's name came up again.

"He told me," Frank said.

"Who told you what?"

"Casey Joe Macbride said he's got a story to tell."

"Well?"

"Why don't you call him; here's his number."

That was that. Frank can be very persuasive with few words. Hell, he ought to be the writer! I did call Casey Joe MacBride and the poems and prose commentaries that follow are his story, or, at least, the first part of it.

He said right away he was no writer. He'd tried more than once but saw immediately that it was not working out his way. He'd read quite a few of my poems in the *Prairie Schooner* over the years, and, yes, he did remember me from college and that I'd worked tree jobs with Dick Groves and sold rick wood all over Shannon County. He knew Frank and I were friends. And he thought I might have some feel for what he wanted set down.

"Having an experience and writing about it are not the same," I said. We'd met in North Platte, Nebraska, halfway between Chadron and Clayton, where he was still teaching History.

"Maybe 'feel' isn't the right word," he said.

I'm not much into feelings. I make up characters and then turn 'em loose to tell their story. If it works, that includes their feelings; if it doesn't, feelings won't make it right.

"You want to take it on?"

"As told to?"

"Yeah."

"Who were those old guys I used to see you with up at Clive and Agnes Guildersleeve's?"

"That was Grandpa and Carlos Little Boy, both younger then than we are now."

"Tell me more."

It took us a while. He's not one-hundred percent satisfied and neither am I. But those ends overlap so that we're about as satisfied as we're ever going to be.

The way the book is set up, even after I'd get the main narrative banged out in blank verse, there was always a thread he'd want to pursue. Well, that led to the prose commentaries. We'd start with the poem's title, then we threw in an epigram or two, something some wise guy had to say about the incident or one tangential to it. Then Casey Joe invariably called back, or, at our next meeting (we continued to meet in North Platte), thought of something more to say about some aspect of the poem he thought deserved more ink.

I said, "Casey, I'm not writing a whole other poem here."

"But this is important! Call it a commentary."

Casey Joe also threw in about halfway through the project that he wanted Kit Watson, a first-rate artist living in Chadron, to add black and white artwork to go along with the poems and commentaries. I had no problem with that. Kit did the mural for the Sandoz Center in Chadron, and after looking at a few preliminaries she sketched, I was more than satisfied.

Hope you enjoy *White River, Vol. I*, by Casey Joe MacBride. And a word more. Greg, will you give me a call? I considered changing your name. But then I didn't.

And another thing. I did not use the names Casey Joe provided unless I received permission first. All other names, while actual, are not the names of anyone involved in any of these narratives. And finally, Casey Joe wanted me to use the Gaelic spelling of his last name (Mac Giolla Bhride).

"Why should it matter?" I asked.

"It's a Donegal name; it matters."

"It'll still be a Donegal name; it'll still matter. St. Brigit will condole. There's Lakota names in here, too; but they're in English. If people want the Irish or the Lakota they can type it into Google."

"Okay."

"Don't forget, bhuicall, until Malcolm asks a doctor early in act four 'Comes the king forth, I pray you?', every word in Macbeth would've been spoken in Gaelic."

"The Irish, is it? That's probably why Donalbain splits to Ireland."

"It is, then. Unlike his brother, he couldn't speak

English."

"Did the witches have the Gaeltacht, too?"

"Double-Gaeltacht, I'm thinking."

"Mmm …."

"Cromwell's moldy kin; count on it."

"It's loonies they are."

"The lot. 'Course on that score, we're all on the rolls."

"Make mine cinnamon," Casey said.

"There's something," I said as we got up to leave. Then the waitress got going on the table (my tip, CJ's turn at the mallard), and with one thing or another it wasn't until I was behind the wheel of my Tundra that I had another chance at Casey Joe. He was about half-way leaning into the cab (leave it to him to not require the running board), and for some reason his right hand had tightened where it straddled the door, just where the center of the window would be if I'd had it up.

"So?"

"So you're all hot and heavy about getting the Irish right. What about your Lakota name … ?" I trailed that one off, though. There was a look in Casey Joe's eye that did not require a whole lot of interpretation, and I turned away, shamed.

"You know better than to ask a thing like that," he said. And he was right; I did. I also knew the only way to leaven our farewell was not to apologize.

-R.F. McEwen
January 2, 2013

Casey Joe's Letter

Dear Bob,

The more I thought about it the more it became important to me to get something in here in my own hand. I came up with this. At first I thought of calling it "Canwape kasna wi," which is October where I come from. It's something like "the month when the wind blows the leaves from the trees." But I settled on "Tracks Don't Lie." It could go in the front; see what you think.

Sincerely,
Casey Joe

I was born in late October
when Fast Horse creek is dry.
The moon shone gaunt through the high forks --
that night my mother died.

And the moon in the creek bed splintered
and the wind began to wail
like the cry of a leg-broke coyote
through my mother's lone travail. ← STANZA BREAK!

It splintered the air with its wailing
and mixed with my mother's cry;
her back twisted in terror
    and blood ran down her thighs.

The cottonwood leaves late October,
the ones that cradled me
where splattered and slick with my birthing
in the bed of Fast Horse Creek.

16   R. F. McEwen

The cottonwood leaves late October,
the ones that cradled me
where splattered and slick with my birthing
in the bed of Fast Horse Creek.

My father was drunk in Rushville;
up north my time had come.
My mother's last cries were joyful --
Grandfather brought me home.

— Casey Joe MacBride

Panaderia

"He kept his head down pretty much at first. And the other students, some, anyway, would give him a rough time. Once he got into his books, though, there was no holding him back. He'd miss a day or two here and there, but to no end. Pretty good with his dukes, too."

Royal Norris, Science Teacher, Chadron City Schools
(1957 – 1972)

W hen I came home from school my second
day
I asked my grandfather about a "breed."
"So what's a 'breed'?" I asked. "Someone said
'breed'."
We'd moved to Chadron down from Fast Horse
Creek
"so he can go to school" my Aunt Rose said.
"He goes up here," my grandfather replied
and turned to Carlos Little Boy for help.
But Carlos shook his head. "Let's get the boy
to Chadron then and see him through," he said.
So there it was; and now we'd come to this.

"It's Mexican for 'bread,' " my grandpa said;
"just like they say 'Let's keel this snake,' instead
of 'kill,' or 'Okayso eef you sayso.'
That's another one; a Mexican will talk
like that, you give him half a chance. Just ask
ol' Carlos, he talks Mexican." "I don't,"
said Carlos Little Boy. "But I know 'breed;'
fried breed is good with any kind of bens."
My grandfather seemed puzzled, but my aunt
went to the kitchen and began to cook.
Much later, after ice cream, she looked down
the table and her jaw relaxed. "I hope,"
she said, "you three have had your fill of 'breeds.'
That's more than one, you know, in Mexican.
In Spanish, you will hear them say 'el pan.'"

R. F. McEwen

This is me trying to burrow into Aunt Rose shortly after she came to live with Grandpa and Carlos Little Boy and me. Carlos and Grandpa were never mean, and they did their best to tone things down. Grandpa took an oath he would not say "God dammit to hell," and Carlos promised to hold the line on Mrs. Critchlow's spending Tuesday and Friday nights over at our place. And although they didn't frighten me nearly as much as my step-mother and father had, there were still moments when I wished someone would come and put things in order. That turned out to be Aunt Rose. I couldn't get enough of her for a long time after she showed up with an over-stuffed World War II Army bag, and a smart way of ordering people around and getting things done.

She smelled of wood smoke and sage even when we didn't keep a fire, and I was always trying to get inside her shawl and up against her, where no one else could come, and be invisible. Whenever Grandpa and Carlos saw me there, they turned away and didn't laugh.

R. F. McEwen

One time Carlos played a trick on Grandpa. It worked because the first two things Grandpa did when he woke up was put his boots on and then cut a plug of Brown's Mule chewing tobacco and stick it in his jaw. Once, I said, "Grandpa why do you like Brown's Mule so much?" and he said, "The juice is walnut-colored like a young eagle's wings." But I never saw him spit.

Stacking Rick Wood: Getting On

"For as long as I was hauling firewood up to Clive
Guildersleeve at Wounded Knee, South Dakota, he was
selling it by the rick, which came out to about a fourth
a' cord, since most wood stoves back then couldn't
handle much more'n a twelve-fourteen-inch piece of
wood. Back here in Crown Point, Indiana, though, a
sixteen-inch log will set up real nice in your fire place.

So here a rick comes out to about one-third of a
cord. It's different in a lot of places."

Don Green; Crown Point, Indiana (1972)

My grandfather and Carlos Little Boy
were right that year the south White River froze
before its time; I think in late November,
nineteen sixty-three. And we'd been cutting
rick wood there, northeast of Chadron, six miles
off the Slim Buttes road; dead ash and elm
(and when my grandfather said "Ellum" we
just grinned). Those times we worked past dark
    we came
prepared with canvas for a lean-to deep
within the grove; then after dark we'd take

some beans and fry bread; coffee, too, and pie.

I couldn't cut then, but I'd rick the wood
and keep the saws in gas and oil, and sharp.
After my parents quit for good six years before,
my grandfather and Carlos Little Boy
kept me in line. We moved to Chadron and
I went to school almost every day.
Most weekends we worked yard jobs, cut rick
    wood;
most summers they both wrangled at Fort Rob
while I stayed back with my aunt Rose. I had
to keep my grades in school, my teachers pleased.
The winter I began this with, we'd worked
Thanksgiving break, then stayed the weekend
    through.
At night the wind pushed hard and had its say.
Upon their faces I could only catch
a sort of cross-cut flashing in the flames,
within their voices only floating bits
that seemed to hang upon the smoke and drift
into a limitless repose. I heard
them once again today, a decade and a half
gone by, on graduation day—I heard
my grandfather and Carlos Little Boy
intone this moment while the river froze.

A Bit More About Ricks

A rick is a measurement of wood eight-feet long, four-feet high, and about a foot to a foot-and-a-half wide. It's maybe one-fourth of a cord. Each piece had to be small and short enough to fit into a wood stove: we didn't cut for fireplaces. People would come into town for wood, or Grandpa and Carlos would haul it up to them, or we'd take it up to Clive and Agnes Guildersleve at Wounded Knee store. Clive was a large man with usually a great laugh inside him waiting to cut loose; his wife, Agnes, a small, business-first woman, could put a dog to shame just by looking at it. She and Aunt Rose were good friends.

This is a stretch of White River as it runs through Slim Buttes, South Dakota. You can see our lean-to and our wood, along with the smoke rising in a thin line from our small fire. You won't find us, though. Grandpa and Carlos and I are down snaking logs out of the river. As you can see, the wood (elm, ash, box elder—ash is best) has not been ricked up yet.

There is another stretch of White River near Crawford, Nebraska, where we sometimes worked wood. Grandpa and Carlos also worked horses at Fort Robinson, west of Crawford, just there on Soldier Creek.

What they did was break horses for tourists to ride. It was a good job or Carlos and Grandpa would not have undertaken it. "Fort Rob makes me break out in hives," Grandfather said.

Carlos said, "I never feel good at Fort Rob, even when they call us in for lunch. I like the foreman, Chuck Canaday, just fine. It's the rest of it I can't negotiate." The "rest of it" took in the bloody footprints that, when you looked keen enough and with everything you had in you, you could still see spread out on the hillside, and all over the parade ground, too. You probably also know what other bloody murder happened there. The parade ground!

Blind Pew

"The way I heard it his mother named him after her brother, Melvin Brings Yellow. But his dad, L. N. Turley, threw in "Bonehead" as his middle name. Sort'a like a joke. Everyone but his dad called him Mel-Bo. And you can read about what happened to Sister Jo. There's some claim they heard her suffercating in one of the back rooms late that night. But what business they'd have out'n about that time, I really can't say."

Clarence Hallmark; Chadron, Nebraska (1962)

"'It's . . . that boy. I wish I had put his eyes out!' cried the blind man, Pew."

Robert Louis Stevenson, *Treasure Island*

I t was a visitor one Wednesday night.
Aunt Rose and Carlos Little Boy had gone
to services at Sister Jo McShane's;
she kept a store-front just across the street
from Dub Long Miller's Favorite Saloon.
And of a night she'd hound the drunks to church
before the services began. She'd shame
them, too, until the meanest of the boys

(one Mel-Bo Turley then) was spirit-caught
and came near crawling to the altar, where
he'd cry for Sister Jo and Jesus both
to mend his suffering and raise his Ma,
who'd died while he was doing eighteen months
in Lincoln for assaulting Richard Bird.
But Sister Jo'd have none of it:
                            "You won't
blaspheme our Savior's house while I'm at home.
Leave my name out; it's Jesus Christ can line
the wayward ramples of a sponge like you,
Bo Turley. A supplicant tonight, is it?
Tomorrow you'll be blind and running loose,
ten times at least as mean. Your mother, son,
would've stumbled on her broken knees to Kyle
and back if sacrifice would keep you out
of town, and dry, and save your soul for Christ.
She would've settled for sobriety
before she died; now, I will, too. The rest
will have to run on luck."

                            Then Bo,
awash in candlelight and penitential tears,
foreswore grain alcohol and white port wine,
foreswore his pals, White River "rats," foreswore
their ways, ungodliness and "lying whores;"
inveighed against Dawes County and a hand
no loving son should hold. He also vowed
to kill his Dad. So Bolin Turley prayed.
Not long and Sister Jo would hear her fill.
She had a plan would keep him warm and out

of Dub Long's alleyway 'til early dawn.
And she would wrap her arms around his chest
and find some hands to help her drag him off
into a side room where she kept some flops
for boys like Melvin and his river rats.
And Carlos Little Boy and my Aunt Rose
were saving sinners then, just pitching in;
they'd sing and ask for pity on the boys
(including me and grandpa, I suspect).
When Bo was squared and soundless on his cot,
his boots beside him on the floor, a quilt
tucked snug beneath his chin, then Sister Jo
would sign the cross, invoke Tunka Shila,
then raise her eyes and, on occasion, cry.

"May I step in?"
                        "I've got to have this boy
to bed. He'll work a book or two, but then
he's got to roll."
                        "I understand. I won't
take too much of your time; and what you give
He will repay ten thousand fold. The boy
will benefit the most, you'll see, in ways
uncountable."
                        "I guess you're in. So, what?
Is that a Testament you're carrying?
Aunt Rose has memorized it through by heart;
maybe not all, but most."
                        "Aunt Rose?"
                                        "Aunt

    Rose.

She's off to church at Sister Jo McShane's
with Carlos. They pray to God and sing;
they're pitching in."
                              "Are you traditionals?
I can't help noticing a feather and
what looks like sage above the crucifix
just there against the wall."
                              "What do you want?
You want a contribution to your church?
Aunt Rose and Sister Jo are coffee sharks;
come back when they're both here, and Carlos,
    too.
They like to spend most of an afternoon
just swilling coffee and discussing God
with preachers who are out collecting dough
and saving souls."
                              "Then, may I come again?
Our souls are in such jeopardy; our hearts
are perishing for sacramental blood,
His perfect love; our prayers, our offerings…."

"Then come again when Sister Jo is here,
and Carlos Little Boy. Aunt Rose will make
fry bread; she'll brew some coffee, bake a pie;
they love to listen while a preacher sets
the world to rights."
                              The man, reluctantly,
I thought, from where I sat over my book
(blind Pew fomenting mischief, and a boy
like me grown anxious that a derelict
and unattending world was drowsing, though

adventures called), then turned to go. He'd hoped
to say another word, but grandpa closed
the door and sighed, then nodded me to bed.

Years later, after everyone was dead,
I read a story in the Journal Star
about how Sister Jo, then eighty-four,
had been murdered while she prayed alone one
    night.
Her niece discovered her. She lay upon
her back, her Bible tucked beneath her head,
the shawl Aunt Rose had made for her too tight
around her throat and covering her face,
so that you couldn't tell if she'd seen Bo
approaching slowly, or recalled him clear.

This is where some people in Chadron went to get drunk. There and at the Buddy Bar around the block. Most often they'd get seed money and chip in for a short pint or even a fifth or a quart if they could come up with the dough. I think a quart of White Port would've been about two-three dollars back then. I should spell it "dolors" not only because of what Aunt Rose said once, that "Nothing ever good comes from drinking yourself blind drunk and making a mess of things in the bargain."

Most often, the guys would get their jug and take it back to the alley where they'd stand in a circle, drink, and pass it on. The first few drops went on to the ground for drinking buddies gone before. Don Roy Little Spotted Horse and I used to hide behind the junk cars and watch them. We wanted to be tough, too, but those men would run us off. And when they saw us they'd tell Grandpa or Carlos, and whichever one they told would come after us with a belt and give us each a good whack, sometimes two. They went after Davey, Don Roy's brother, too, even when he wasn't there.

Mel-Bo Turley didn't mind getting boys drunk, though. But one time Grandpa and Carlos got him against the wall, and when he tried to act tough, Carlos laid him out with one of his crutches.

Even in winter, you'd see guys passed out back there in the alley with usually a bunch of women and kids going through their pockets for the grocery or rent money.

The Lessoning

"All we heard was that after he did his time in Pierre, her youngest brother went down into Illinois where he expected to keep away from troublemakers and stay by himself and do right. His sister and Mildred Cross brought the coffin back to Chadron on the Chicago-Northwestern, ((And the)) station wagon back up to Porcupine. Darnell Slaughterdown said, 'Hell of a ways to go just to get snake bit.' Even so, tore everyone up pretty good that time, I can tell you that."

Floyd Cummings; Pine Ridge, South Dakota (1953)

I undertook one time (I must've been near
    eight)
to set a bull snake loose inside our house.
I thought because Aunt Rose was in her years
and bred along the river, she would know
a bull against a rattler anyway,
and not get sore.

                        But Carlos Little Boy
and Grandpa came back early from Slim Buttes
before I had the chance to get things said.
Those days we spelled each other at the tub,

and who went next would have to wait his turn
a good half-hour before another pail
was boiling on the kitchen stove.

                              Aunt Rose
bathed three-four times a week and took her
     time.
Grandpa and Carlos Little Boy and I
just once: but more when they'd bucked spuds
in Hemingford. They'd start their bath outside
(I worked the pump) then take their turn inside.
Two towels would hold us through the week;
     Aunt Rose
used three: I'll let that be.

                              Not many years
past then, we bought a water heater and began
to use it regular. Whenever we
were burdened by a heavy snow, and stayed
too long out shoveling, we got in line.
And when they'd been out cutting ash wood,
working horses, stacking hay, they yearned to
     soak.
We all agreed hot water with some salts
would loosen joints, unravel mysteries.
We also knew there was a place inside
that salt and water couldn't find.

                              That time
I set the bull snake loose, I didn't know
Aunt Rose had lost her brother when a moccasin
bit through his shirt while they were visiting
along Big Muddy, deep in Illinois.
They'd walked into the red oak woods, too far

for her to drag him out. And so she stood
a witness while his shoulder swelled, his throat,
his face and, finally, she watched his skin
split ragged while his blood spread bubbling
and black upon her chest. She'd closed his eyes.

This is the house we lived in when we moved to Chadron in 1953. The pump and wash tub are around back. The shack at the left is where Grandpa and Carlos had to stay when they came home too late. I wanted to go in there, too. Aunt Rose called it the "Bunk" house. After I stayed out there for a while and listened to what Carlos and Grandfather told each other, I understood why. Over time, Grandpa and Carlos stayed home most nights. When we ran short of meat, though, they'd be out and about up north with flashlights and rifles. Then, if they lucked out, even if they came in early the next morning or late the next day, they wouldn't have to stay in the bunk house except to bleed and skin and butcher game. Then clean up after.

Aunt Rose's Rummaging

"I know because we used to go into Bannock
country diggin' spuds. They made a team, those two.
Out drink, out ride, out work, out fight and out what-
ever else you could come up with, anyone within twen-
ty miles. But once they took on the boy and moved
down to Dawes County, they put the brakes on. You
wouldn't hear a word against either one. I think she was
always a little bit touchy, though, about them fallin' off
the road side, if you know what I mean."

> Loren Dean Weston, Manderson, South Dakota
> (1962)

> "I left my peaceful residence
> A foreign land to see
> I bid adieu to Donegal
> Likewise to Glen Swilly"
>> Irish Immigration Song

By that time of the afternoon, Aunt Rose
had had about enough of me. She'd been
since seven in the morning hot to get
three years of rummage sorted for the sale

she planned for Saturday, and here it was
the Thursday afternoon before. Next day
was taken with Teresa Black Bull's trip
to see her wounded brother in Pine Ridge,
then back to Chadron with commodities.
Grandpa and Carlos almost had to write
their names in blood to be back Friday night
before she calmed enough to let them head
up north for branding—and that was Tuesday
    night.

"There might be something when the branding's
    done,"
I heard Aunt Rose tell Grandpa late that night.
"Connealy always has some fence to mend,
some thing or other he won't do himself.
You tell him 'No;' and tell him 'No' for two.
I don't want Carlos left alone up there;
his uncle Theodore will hear you're gone
and swoop down like a hungry boomer hawk
and set him off. Remember last July
when Carlos spent a week in Sheridan
for breaking Charlie Silvernagle's arm
then calling Randall's deputy some names
he won't forget? Besides, RoxAnn won't hold
her place for long." Aunt Rose was careful to
neglect a "Come straight home." She knew the
    more
you say, sometimes, the worse you didn't want
to happen might, and teach you tact too late.
Much later, after Grandpa went to bed,

it took the door and then his shuffling
to tell me Carlos Little Boy was home.

That day at school had been the last before
our long-awaited summer break, and I
had more sublime adventures in my head
than Chadron held. Each postponed camping trip
Grandpa and Carlos promised would be ours
when school was out; our trips to Wounded Knee
to visit Clive and Agnes Guildersleeve;
my swimming in the river at Slim Buttes;
the visiting with relatives once lost,
now rediscovered when our "Missing" ad
was answered late in April; and the whole
of unencumbered summer's times, like bees
were loose inside my head. I couldn't sleep.
So I heard Carlos at the door; I heard
his shuffling, his effort to convince
whoever was awake he wouldn't wake
a slumberer outside of fire. Aunt Rose
was waiting, though, with walnut-marble cake
and fresh-brewed coffee straight from Maxwell's
        house.
She asked about his sister's suffering
to spend lost time at Chadron Hospital
until the swelling just beneath her arm
was diagnosed as something they could treat
at home. That's where he'd been since eight
        o'clock
and I could tell by how his voice kept trailing off
then catching, he was inconsolable.

And so Aunt Rose did not pursue his grief.
She knew the story of their parents' death
and how his sister took the children on
when she was seventeen, and they were twelve,
eight, five and three. There was a sweat
the night before they brought her down from
Manderson. But morning came too soon
and Carlos and his younger brother said,
along with Jonas Spotted Elk, who'd cut
the wood, and Wilber Lame, who'd led, to get
her down to Chadron where Aunt Rose could see
she had good care. And Carlos' sister, too,
who's blue-green eyes were sharp as whittled ash
said it was best, since everything'd been done,
to take her down.

                  And now they wondered when
Doc Cerny would agree to send her home.
Their voices were subdued to whispering
and sounded like the shudder of the moths
against my screen to get inside. I dozed,
then woke to urgency in Aunt Rose's voice.
She said she knew the branding was a thing
they'd signed for and she had no problem there.
"He's always generous," she said. "And when
my dad was running cattle up that way,
Connealys always could be counted on
to throw and brand a bawling calf. Of course,
we knew, and they did, too, there always were
a few on either side that strayed (were drove?
no one would ever say) into a draw

or down along the bottom when French Creek
turns sand in August and the wandering
begins, that somehow came to show a brand
that had no business in the light of day."
It wasn't like Aunt Rose was testifying;
and Carlos was a hand who wasn't shy
about a transformation here and there
which nature, as he'd sworn while Jesus slept,
intended when Connealys "started first."
"It's just something I'll say," she said. "They'll
       have
more work to do, some nonsense left undone
since Jericho; not worth the doing, though,
the sort of thing you'd rather have complete,
but can't stir up the where-with-all to do."
When Carlos Little Boy acknowledged this,
she started speaking slow. "You know ol' Gramps
is always looking for the ways and means
to keep our heads above, so we can live
in town and keep things clear for Swisher Sweet
(a name she used sometimes because of when
my face turned green from smoking Gramp's
       cigar)
with school and all, and later when he's set and
on his own."

                    I wouldn't know that night
what Aunt Rose meant. I had a terror then
of waking in an empty house: the fire
was long past smoldering, the ashes cold
and insignificant; the table cloth

was soiled; wojapi sludge and greenish lumps
of last week's bread were moldering in bowls
set for a breakfast by an empty hand.
I saw three rats; their eyes were mocking me.
I saw a fourth; its eyes were walled and red.
And I knew then Aunt Rose and Carlos, both,
Grandfather, too, had died and left me lorn
and naked in a nasty, treacherous,
wind-sharpened place, without a quilt or crust
of comfort, or the breath of love at all.
That night I caught my breath and heard Aunt
    Rose
go on, "But we'll see clear. Don't scrabble so.
I need you boys back home for rummage work
this Saturday. The lot will have to go,
and I'll need help. I'll need to see you both
this Friday night. You'll have to pull Gramps off
whatever horse he's on and get the two
of you back here. Especially—look here—
if RoxAnn's coming home. And Carlos, mind,"
(she tried to leave this as an afterthought
but drilled it home instead) "why don't you drive.
Grandpa should come straight home, and so
    should you.
We know how he'll just talk himself into
an awful way: how everything's a mess
so what's the use? Not maybe in those
words, but… well, just straight back home
and carry horses to the front, cross-boards,
then rummage. Afterwards, we'll count the loot
and maybe get ol' Roxie home to die."

When Friday afternoon was closing in,
we found a folded paper underneath
an old cigar box used for clips and keys.
When Aunt Rose opened it, she shushed me off
and found a chair, but I hung back to watch.
And I could see Aunt Rose's eyes begin
to cloud, although they didn't overflow.
After she set the paper down, she said,
"I want those crates up from the basement now,
and don't forget the light." When I returned
well-stocked with rummage, I noticed that the
        hands
were gaining on the point Grandfather said
to count on Carlos and himself for hauling
horses out, and plywood squares, and signs
and price-tabs, too, and rummage in large crates,
and baskets heaped with winter rags and socks
and mittens, and some sorry quilts Aunt Rose
insisted were past due. And then I saw
the note.
            "Dear Glen Swilly," it started with
(the place my great-grandfather lived before
he was sent off to South Dakota as a boy,
a sign pinned to his collar, and no one
to speak his Irish but a priest at Sharp's,
a Jesuit named Father Art), "please tell
your Aunt we'll both be home in time to help.
We're well along the Slim Buttes road by now;
in fact, we just passed Johnny Weasel Bear's;
the dust is thick, ungodly, and our throats
are swole and burning, son; we're mighty dry.

And we are drowned in drought, but we don't
    care;
we're heading at a steady clip for home.
Connealy had at least ten-thousand bucks
apiece if we stayed on to wrestle hogs,
but we said 'No!' And we forgot who slipped
the word in we might want to stop before
we undertook our dusty drive back home,
but to that implication we said 'No!'
Please tell Aunt Rose, Glen, we're coming home.
And ask her to inquire of Roxie Ann."

R. F. McEwen

Aunt Rose set planks across saw horses in the front yard and sold rummage. She never sold children's clothes, though. Once Delores Jenks came all the way down to Chadron from Red Shirt Table and said, "Aunt Rose, there are some scrappy boys and girls up on the Table who are not ready for winter." Aunt Rose said, "Come back in two weeks." Then we went door-to-door in Chadron, then west to Crawford and east to Hay Springs and Rushville. Pickings were slim in Crawford and Hay Springs. When the two weeks were up, she about had those scrappy boys and girls up on Red Shirt Table ready for winter.

My Great-Great Uncle's Passed

"I think he'd a' gotten her into the obituaries any-
way, even when he'd promised Winston to let it go.
Quite a few at both ends already knew. Maybe that's
why her brother did what he did: he was ashamed she'd
be with someone who felt shamed to be with her. They
got him, though; then cut him down not three weeks
into thirty years to life."

Elston Barrens; Gordon, Nebraska (1948)

When Winston Slaughterdown got spider bit
last August south of Rushville where he ran
his traps, a mile this side of Split Pine Creek
just where the cottonwood turns into ash,
he made his brother swear to set him deep
within the ground he'd kept prepared those six-
    teen years
since Minnie Quiver died. "Northeast," he said,
"a mile below the bluff where Richard's trap line's
lost in Shannon County, where she bled
to death the night her brother watched us both
in love then slipped out of the shade and cut
her throat." "I know it, then," his brother said.

By now, my uncle's tongue was cracked and blue,
and when he'd go to breathe his cheeks collapsed.
But still, "Don't stick us in the papers, Dan,"
he rasped, like someone rolling muddy in a ditch.
"No papers… still," his brother said, "it won't
make any difference; she's dead. And you'll
be, too." Then Winston Slaughterdown began
to twist, and when his shoulders stopped his head
dropped sideways in his brother's lap, and then
his wall eye, as it settled into place
held steady on his brother till the two
were shut from daylight by a line of clouds
that, passing, left the left eye still in darkness
when it caught within a crease that wouldn't close.

This is Winston Slaughterdown's last Will and Testament. If you read it, you'll know why it was tied up in probate for so long and why his brother was so mad at Minnie Quiver's daughter, who ended up with over half the two-year-olds (which her mother would've had if her own rotten brother had not come out of the shadows and cut his sister's throat). But then Jack Clausen signed on for a share, and after three weeks of everybody hitting below the belt, the court finally came to his conclusion.

If Winston Slaughterdown had more time, he might have reconsidered the entire arrangement. But who thinks he'll get spider-bit and die a mile this side of Split Pine Creek, cradled by a brother he can't stand? It's a long way to Tipperary! Anyway, as things were, the will reads, "and in the event. . ." And it didn't take much of an imagination to figure that one out—and a good part of both Sheridan and Shannon counties will bear me out on this: there had been talk.

So whatever papers Winston was so concerned about would not have changed much as far as either the daughter or the law were concerned.

In any case, when Mildred Cross finally had her due, everyone said, "And we all know what she'll do with it." But she didn't. No sir! She followed Aunt Rose's brother to down-state Illinois and bought into a horse ranch. She did well, too, and sometimes sent a full-broke yearling back for a funeral or a naming, or for a veteran returning or just setting out. Aunt Rose said, "We will call her 'Weya sunka wakan ota yu ha win.'"

Buried Deep at Fast Horse Creek

"It was a pretty rotten day all around. That's what I heard; and how you could see it different will remain an eternal mystery to me. Then while it was working itself out to no good end, a few of 'em decided to duck in under the congestion and settle old scores. That's another thing I heard."

"But there's no record of that happening."

"Well, maybe it didn't then. I'm just saying. Be about as much blood either way, I guess."

Overheard by Justin Marshall in Crawford, Nebraska
(1943)

One night I asked Grandfather if we might
explore the ground just south of Porcupine
for arrowheads. "The Boy Scouts went up there
and found a bunch," I said. "The Boy Scouts?
    Where?"
he asked. "From Middle School. The Boys
    Scouts, Gramps.
They're on the go; they hike and camp around;
they do their crafts." "Their crafts is it," he said;

"who's heading up the craft department now?"
"The science teacher, Mr. Norris, Gramps;
Mr. Norris is the leader of the Scouts.
He had them south of Porcupine, they said,
last April; now again this coming May."
"I hope they don't get poked," Grandfather said.
"It may be Carlos has a relative
up there can keep them clear of diamondbacks,
and bed the Scouts down nice and cozy where
they'll find a decent sleep."
                                        But Carlos heard,
just coming in from Goodman's Produce where
he'd gone for bleach and suds. "We've got
a day to go to work and hang and fold,"
he said, "against Aunt Rose's return. And she'll
inveigh against us sure if we slack off.
You both have got more relatives up there
than me; I won't abide a rusty bolt
to shut me in. I say it's back-stabbers
and worse up there." "It's arrowheads this time,"
Grandfather said; "Boy Scouts are on the trail.
Don't sell the science teacher short; don't turn
all sour against your blood."

                                        Although he smiled,
although there was no anger in his voice,
there was an edge, and Carlos turned his eyes
to Grandfather's and held them there for what
seemed over-long. It took some time before
I came to reckon what I wasn't told,
until my reckoning exceeded what

I was. "There's blood to go around," he said,
"there's not an arrowhead or bone they'll find
that won't be bloody, broke or ripped apart.
I say to let'm be." I looked at my
grandfather, then to Carlos Little Boy,
and felt between them something hanging like
the echo of a wounded hawk, the sound
the wind made up at Fast Horse Creek the day
they buried Carlos' sister, Pearl, when I
was only four years old and bundled in
a quilt, then set within a little grove
of frozen, waist-high grass that stood between
the burying and me. Her son, Sylvester, drove
each nail into the cedar boards, each ring
of steel-on-steel exploding down the creek
like single shots, or lone and single barks
a grievous-wounded dog will make before
all hope is gone and death is nigh; and when
the keening caught the air, the wind began
to slice down from the ridge and make its moan
a naked voice among the rest. And I
was cold that time, despite Aunt Rose's voice,
which caught the wind and shook it like she
        would
a musty shawl. And, when I think of it,
though deep in August (the Moon of Ripening,
when we would damp the ground beneath our
        quilts
and sleep out back when breathing was a chore
inside the house)—no matter where I am,
no matter now though forty years are gone

since I sat lorn and chilled and terrified
surrounded by sharp stands of frozen grass,
Sylvester's pounding and his mother gone,
each nail exploding in the cedar planks,
exploding down the twisting, barren length
of Fast Horse Creek, and in the quaking heart
of me, and with the keening and the wind,
relentless, wave-on-wave, and me in mute
debilitation while my relatives
exalted in the futile massacre
of everything that lives—I say a chill
strikes deep within me like a piece of steel
against a lethal edge of flint, and in
that sound, in each reverberation, gaunt,
quick, sharp and clean, my blood congeals in sad-
        ness
in the fathomless night chambers of my soul.
Aunt Rose would not allow a bitterness
to breed; "The time for tears is short," she'd say,
"blind Angus threads his needles by himself
and beads without a light."
                                    "Those arrowheads
will have to burrow deeper in the bank,"
Grandfather said, "or else the Scouts will catch
the lot and mount them on the nearest wall."
"The nearest Wall's a further stretch up north,"
said Carlos; "they sell pills and crafts. And when
you come on time you get free coffee, too."
With this the kitchen air began to clear
like any sky would of an afternoon
when storm clouds threatening dispersed, or like

a bitter soul would clear when suddenly
enraptured in a long, unreckoned bliss. "At least
I hope they ask permission first, those Scouts,"
said Carlos then.

              "Who from?" I asked him,
but he disappeared into the basement where
we heard him rummaging with this and that.
My grandfather was smiling, though. My eyes
in consternation caught him struggling
to keep his mouth from fracturing in mirth.
Then Carlos' feet were heavy on the stairs.
He held the laundry basket, and he huffed,
"Let's make some suds and hang a load before
the afternoon plays out. Just sitting here
we're tempting wrath and I know who will win."

This is an arrowhead one of the Boy Scouts found up near Wounded Knee. His name is Dan Driscoll. He said, "Maybe you can tell us something about this?" I took it home and showed it to Grandpa and Carlos. They said, "It's an arrowhead; it goes in easy and comes out hard." And that's what I told Dan Driscoll.

There was not much Grandpa and Carlos Little Boy couldn't do on horseback.

Carlos Little Boy is Set Upon

"No one knew what it was about. The one with
the crutches was getting in some fairly sound licks until
three or four of 'em swarmed him. Some claim Merlin
Twiss had a pliers, but I didn't see that. When the old
man got into it, though, everyone scattered. He'd make
you cry 'uncle' in short order, that one would."

Clyde Beemish, Chadron, Nebraska (1954)

Grandfather said that time he broke one back
he could've broken twelve. "Six-hundred if
you like," he said; "there wasn't where-with-all
in Shannon county to extinguish me."
He said, "They had him down to where his arm
was pinned behind him and his knees jammed up
against his chest. And Merlin Twiss here'd caught
a-holt of Carlos' ear with pliers, and in
the heat he would'a sideways ripped it off
except I clapped onto his back and caught
his neck a good one with a length of chain
that's left its mark til now." And there was Twiss,
Frank Merlin Twiss, his eyes alight with mirth
and mischief, yanking down his blue bandana,

past a line of flairing purple splayed across
three lumpy veins and disappearing in
his collar just behind his neck. "He'd give
that chain a bite," Frank Merlin said. "You might
say 'Give a Twiss a twist,' " opined Aunt Rose.
I learned much later it had taken more
than months of sweat and moderation for
Aunt Rose to stare down malice for a Twiss,
especially for this one here, who'd been,
as she had seen it then, the where-with-all
whereby her uncle Herbert Nickodemus lost
his battle with his manhood, and became
a drunk for life which, thanks to Merlin Twiss
and Talbot, too, did not last long
once he returned from South Korea blown
the wrong side out. "Those dogs ran Uncle
      down,"
she'd have it understood throughout the day
she toiled to bury Uncle Herbert in
an early autumn rain storm turned to sleet.
Now, in the kitchen, I remembered how
the wind caught Reverend Swallow's braids and
      set
them, ice-tipped, flailing wild and bitter like
two raging snakes; and that I'd sent in one
great heave my puny shovel-full of mud
into his face instead of in the hole,
and bolted, shamed, self-crucified, and lamed
with insignificance.

                              She said, "He drank

himself to death then died on fire." For it
was true; there hadn't been much left of him
to sweep into the little cedar box
they had from Crow, the undertaker, who
advised the family to drive him up
to Sturgis for a military cross.
Instead, they set him in the hollow where
the rise behind their great-grandfather's stone
dips slant-ways into thistle and wild rose.

From what Frank Merlin Twiss remembered, first
the lamp, and then the toe of Uncle's boot
caught Merlin's brother flush against his head
and sent him spinning toward the pallet where
Aunt Rose's nephew, Albert, was asleep.
The lantern, too, went spinning 'til it smashed
in one great flame against the Linwood stove.
Then, Uncle Herbert had Frank Merlin down
and nearly smothered with his forearm in
his mouth. "Unless I'd clamp my jaws, my breath
was gone," Twiss said, as if he only now
just understood how Uncle Frank's fresh blood,
some nearly dried, was sharp inside
his mouth and caked all up along his cheeks
and chin when Scoon McGoins and that boy
of his (the one they called "Jack Shorn") pulled
him and Albert (who'd burrowed into him)
beyond the lick of flame that jumped the door.
Now Merlin mumbled how he'd gone back twice:
"The first, he'd wave his skinning blade so close
he nearly dressed me down. 'It's not your day,'

he screamed, 'I'll dress you down.' 'Ili waste,'
I screamed; 'Waste lo,' Herbert said then fell away.
I thought he might come back at me when I
tried Talbot's collar but they rolled against
a wall and only stared."

                              Frank Merlin Twiss
went on to keep the rest inside. We knew
what happened: it was just like Aunt Rose said;
her Uncle Herbert Nickodemus drank
himself to death then died on fire. And it
was all Frank Twiss could do to get the boy
outside, then try again for Talbot and
for Uncle Herbert just before the roof
collapsed. They'd all been drinking hard that day
and running back and forth to Scenic,
starting fights and laying drunk and waking up,
then throwing down again.
                              He'd lived to tell;
after that time, he never drank again.
"Your brother Talbot drank himself to death,
then died on fire," Aunt Rose accounted (near
to whispering she was). She touched her hand
to Frank's right shoulder then, and as one
     smooths
a twisted patch of brow, she spread her hand.

Our kitchen almost seemed to waft upon
the darkening evening like a floating wing,
or like the lung-deep breathing in a sleep
well-earned will linger when the moths retire

yet keep a vigil there, just where the night
dissolves in daylight's fire. Just how, or when,
or where Grandfather may have fractured some
    one's back
when Carlos Little Boy (he said) was down,
our wonderment with Frank Twiss' scar, his mirth
turned mute, and then in distance lost, Aunt
    Rose's
simmering, her broken voice, her calm dissolve,
her absolution, clear and clean, the sound
of Grandpa recollecting in his sleep
some moment past or still to come that caused
his sleep to be melodious without
a sound: all this and more is less a time
I will remember later on, then what
is ever living, still, and breathing deep.

The way I heard much later is that the McGoin's faction started calling them dog-eaters because of his son's long hair, which, by the time he was ten or eleven years old, was down to his waist. His father didn't much care, but his mother was tearing hers out. The Methodists were down on the transitionals, she said, and she intended to remain in the congregation for the duration and get herself buried decent on the hillside behind the church. And she didn't want any nonsense about it, either, except maybe Reverend Hollow Horn eulogizing her in Lakota just before the giveaway. "He owes us from a long way back," she said.

But McGoin himself became desperate when some of the notes he had out ended up due at the same time. He'd decided to hold his yearlings back, then lost sight of the hay situation. She'd begged him not to get them any more extended than they already were, but he caught her when her back was turned and closed the deal. And now he could feel Lon Binkman over at the First National in Rushville breathing fire down his back. If he could only make the interest, he believed he could put him off until her land sale (which she was not aware of yet) went through. He had about three-quarters socked away but needed more, and her brother was no longer open to suggestions.

All at once then, Scoon started dragging the boy out more and more to feed stock and check fence. He'd send Darnell out across the field and, while he was gone, pour out a bit of his soda and add just a bit of hooch back in. Then a bit more each time, until one late afternoon Darnell went blank on the far side of the cab, tangled in his bibs and hair.

Scoon drove them up to Rapid City then, and sold his own son's hair to a beautician friend of his who'd been in it from the start. And that's how the boy got the name "Jack Shorn."

From then on, he shaved his head every morning. And you could see the scrapes and gouges where he'd been in a hurry or a rage. I asked him before I knew better, "Jack Shorn, why won't you stop shaving your head and let your hair grow out and slick't back with Brill Cream?"

"My name's not Jack Shorn," he shouted, "or are you crazy?" Then he knocked back his shoulders and marched off. Fifteen years later, he came back from Khe Sanh with a Purple Heart and a Silver Star. He needed help, though, with his wheel chair.

Scoon was off somewhere; the ranch was gone, and Reverend Hollow Horn had granted his mother's wish. By then, he'd quit shaving his head. Although he never walked again, he did go on to become a first-class auctioneer. He started his own outfit: Darnell's Running-Smooth Auction and Appraisals. Even worked his dad into it.

R. F. McEwen

You wouldn't know Carlos Little Boy was crippled up. He'd lost his feet when he was only a boy hiding under a hay stack during a blizzard near Loneman. He was so cold when he crawled in there that he never knew his feet were sticking out. For three days, he was under there before Davis High Hawk, who'd gone out to check stock, dragged him out. Here is the hay stack; it has stopped snowing, so you can see his feet.

Aunt Rose in Great Demand

"The Thompsons were wild and mean. They'd go up and down the Slim Buttes road doing just about whatever came their way. And I'm not putting any restrictions on that, either. Once when Lucius Iron Rope. . . well, just take my word. Leave it to Dan Connor to get two of 'em, though, down in Chadron. Put multiple holes in each one."

Nelson Roan Eagle, Slim Buttes, South Dakota
(1953)

If ever I would write about my aunt,
I'd have to mention her Lakota hymns
and how the mourners from as far away
as Kyle and Porcupine sent down for her
when we moved down to Chadron Labor Day
of 1953. From Manderson
they'd send; from Mission and from Wounded
    Knee;
from Fast Horse Creek, and Oglala, too;
from Red Shirt Table mourners sent for her,
and from Pine Ridge, sometimes Potato Creek.
Slim Buttes held out, though, for a couple years

because, as grandpa said:

                          "They kept a grudge
from when Aunt Rose's father's cows got clear
and caused an accident three miles this side
of Johnny Weasel Bear's; a little boy was hurt
and later died. Aunt Rose's father'd tried
to make things right, but everyone took sides
and things were said. Then someone dumped a cow
into the river north of Felix Frog's
and covered it with willow brush and logs,
and when it started rotting in the spring
the stink washed through the whole White River south
of Frog's. And you could taste that stink, and when
the Little Spotted Horses found the hide
it bore the Connor's 'Lonesome J.' The law
convened but couldn't find. Then Carlos here
heard Alvey Thompson's boy one night in town
back of the Favorite big-mouthing with
a pint of Ancient Age. After a few,
he bragged they'd turned the circus loose, his dad
and him, and that they meant, when Rose's dad
was in the pen, to grab his land, his stock,
rock-bottom, and his new windrower, too.
But when Carlos told his uncle Dan,
Dan knocked him down and tied him to a tree."

That's all grandpa would say. But during weeks
and months and years of bits and pieces there,

I learned Aunt Rose's father drove to town
and found those two while they were drinking
    beer
at Buddy's Bar and shot them dead. Their heirs
still got the land, though, when Dan Connor tried
to break the pen in Lincoln and was crucified
with twelve more years.
                        Aunt Rose's mother was
a Kills at Night, and when she had to sell
their land to pay the bank, and, all too soon,
the funeral expenses, she began
to wander out along the Slim Buttes road
and throw whatever came to hand at passing cars.
"You have no relatives," she'd scream in Sioux,
or in what French she knew. The day she died
Aunt Rose and Carlos roamed their stretch to
    coax
her (drag, if necessary) off the road.
The wind was up that latter-end of day
in mid-July, and dust as sharp as glass
caught in their eyes, so that they couldn't see
her when she stepped into a load of yearling
    steers.

It wasn't just Aunt Rose's voice; she sang
old-style, and often made my grandpa cry;
but only when she sang around the house.
The elders wouldn't cry at funerals,
unless it pained inside too much to hold their
    grief.
Then all they needed was Aunt Rose, her voice,

her old-time way of cradling their pain
and rocking it to sleep another day.
She'd sing old-timey gospel music, too.
And Carlos Little Boy and I would beg her
after dinner and the give-away
to sing some Maybelle Carter, then some Hank.
And so she'd give us "Wildwood Flower," and
    then
"I Saw the Light."
                    And then, approaching day
on our way home along the Slim Buttes road,
one of her favorites, Hank's "Lost Highway."

Buvez de l'ean de White River.
Petites gorge´s jusquea´ ce que
vous s'habituer a' elle. Il vous fera
tenir debout.

Elle essai de nous
empoisoner. ALLONS-Y.

A lot of people did not realize Aunt Rose spoke French. Her mother spoke some, but she was a Shangreau, so I'm supposing it came natural to her. After I studied a bit in school, I understood that most of what Aunt Rose's mother spoke was just sounds and syllables that sounded like she knew what she was doing. She'd say "This is a Bordeaux accent," then come out with something. Or, "This is how they ask for wojapi in Marseilles," and then do that for a while.

Aunt Rose, though, had been to the Sisters and could really do it right (as you can see from the picture). It's what I call "Aunt Rose Speaks French." I found out about her prowess in foreign languages when three distant relatives visited up at Porcupine for several weeks. They had come from France and were claiming enrolled, blood status going back to Eugene Little Soldier, which wouldn't have gotten them any credit with the folks up at Standing Rock. They spoke French so well we couldn't understand a word they said, except Aunt Rose and Father Jack, a Jesuit from American Horse Creek who knew a lot of languages.

There were two women and a man. One of the women looked like Mary Alice Charging Thunder, the other one looked like Betty Crocker. The man was about Aunt Rose's age with very black eyes and hair and skin like baking powder. Whatever Aunt Rose said he thought was funny. When they came down to Chadron they were interested in the French street names and in all the food Aunt Rose cooked. By that time, Aunt Rose could keep up with them pretty well. Grandpa and Carlos Little Boy and I felt left out. Carlos said, "I hope they leave." Grandpa added, "Pronto, Tonto." Seems like he had a way with languages, too. But not French.

One of the reasons we were becoming vexed was because Aunt Rose offered our beds (which they jumped at—I should say "in") while we went out to the bunk house. Before we knew it, they were eating all our food. Grandpa had to go up to Wounded Knee for commodities. They liked the cheese. And, even though they drank a gallon a day until they were falling out all over the place, they claimed not to care for either Thunderbird or Richards' Wild Irish Rose. They called it "Reeshaaards." And when they did, Grandpa whispered "Retreads."

The morning of the third day, the guy came down to breakfast with his lower jaw tied up in a blue rag. He was pretty mad, too. You could see it in his eyes; they blazed. And even though he did his mumbling in French, we got his drift. And in ten minutes, they'd cleared out, the lot. They would've "borrowed" our truck, too, but Carlos ran out and snatched the keys from the ignition, so they ended up walking the four blocks to the Trailways.

All that time we didn't see Aunt Rose, but after

they were off, she came skipping down the stairs with a look of merriment in her eyes and her right fist tied in a large, white rag that smelled like liniment.

This is Sampson Bearkiller leaning against the truck the winter he worked with Grandpa and Carlos Little Boy. Sampson Bearkiller could lift that truck if he wanted to, and the next winter he got a chance when he and his son Frank and I got caught in the gumbo down along the White River at Slim Buttes, South Dakota, just south of Felix Frog's. When we were down there in that gumbo, we saw a World War I Army tent and the two families who had been living in it through the winter.

When I told Carlos Little Boy about it, he said it reminded him of the long winter his uncle Ansel and his cousins stayed cold up north just east of the turn–off.

"The turn–off; where's that?"

"Don't press me," he said, "It was a long, cold winter."

"How cold?"

"Pretty cold."

R. F. McEwen

This is the watch Grandpa said I would have after he was dead. He kept another pocket watch nailed to the headboard on his bed that was all cracked up and had been moribund for a long time. Grandpa said a bull "tramped it." "Why didn't you keep it in your pocket with a chain like you do this one?" and I pointed to the bulge in his front jean watch pocket. "I did," he said. "The watch never left my pocket." That's when I learned how Grandpa came to limp and how his watch got wrecked.

Wowahwala

Casey Joe told me this story early on. I took it as a side-line, but he's yanking at my arm to work it in. Wowahwala is "Humility" in the Lakota hierarchy of virtues, one hard gained.

-R.F.M.

I did feel more than proud about loading the truck all by myself after I came home from school one late November day in 1954, about a half year after we moved down to Chadron. When I came in after school, Aunt Rose told me Carlos Little Boy was still broken up about his cousin Sandy Miner and the mess she'd gotten herself into out west in Crow country, and he was moping it up out in the bunk house.

Grandpa's long overdue date with the dentist had left the inside of his jaw so lacerated he couldn't do much without it flaring into a brush fire. (Aunt Rose remarked she would not hazard her teeth with someone who got most of his revenue cutting hair.) So he was in the bunk house, too, trying to sit still and keep his mouth shut (which was not easy given Carlos' passion for casting his grief in a wide arch, making it more sustainable for himself—Aunt Rose said once, "Carlos Little Boy will drag you in" and she was right). So every two-three minutes you'd hear Grandfather's groaning, loud and lingering, the last the introduction to the next, and the next the conclusion to the last, each groan receding like a stricken dog's last howl . . . well, maybe not that bad . . . still.

Aunt Rose said after I had my pie I might think about loading the truck because Grandpa and Carlos had to deliver wood all the way up to Sharp's Corner, and neither was in any kind of shape to put a load together. Dick Groves, a railroader and tree trimmer both, occasionally left logs in our back yard to save himself a trip to the dump. When that happened, all Carlos and Grandpa had to do was buck, split, load, and haul. Well, now this wood was ripe to load.

I marked the way Aunt Rose just threw out about me "thinking about it." Anyone could see how puny I was at eight years old, and she knew how difficult it would be for me to lift the split quarters of locust and ash up to the tail gate, then stack them just so to make a full load. She'd turned back to the cupboard, though. When she asked if I'd seen the powdered milk I knew we would have smashed potatoes for supper. I got out without answering, though, and without her looking back.

It would be two to three hours later and near full-dark when I came tramping back into the kitchen with my jacket over my shoulder and my sleeves rolled high on my arms, where wood trash, mud, and scrapes and gouges testified to my recent scuffle with that load.

And I was sweating, too (that wasn't drizzle dripping from my chin); and I made my chest big by drawing my shoulders back and holding my breath.

"Well, I dusted that off pretty good," I tossed out, hoping. . . oh, I don't know what; maybe that Aunt Rose would fall prostrate on the linoleum and have ten-twelve coronaries (Carlos Little Boy said "canaries") before she found her way back to her feet and fell all over me, concurrent with her begging to know what I required for dessert. But all she said was, "Don't think of washing up in the kitchen, Mr. Titus Livermore! Hose off in the yard, then drop into the basement and bring up a full pail of Murphys."

Where was the recognition, the respect, the awe, the gratitude? Where was the benediction; the headlong avalanche of bravos, guaranteed to raise your chin and swell your chest, to lengthen every stride you took until the end of time? When I returned from the yard, I headed straight for the basement; Aunt Rose didn't look up from her work, and I didn't look back (except out of the far-left corner of my weather-eye) before I made a racket going down the stairs.

As I filled the pail, I heard Grandpa and Carlos come in from the bunk house; I heard them take their chairs at the table, and I heard Carlos' chair crack as he leaned it back into the wall. "You'll break that one day," I heard Aunt Rose say, "and the splintered slats will penetrate your lungs before you hit your head against the wall. You'll die messy and imploring forgiveness for all your rotten ways past, present, and to come. But no one will hear you, Gunga Flynn. We'll all be having a grand ol' time for ourselves at the Dawes County Fair while you're lying here in the middle of the floor with pine-slat splinters protruding from your rib cage and your words, like moths around an open flame, fluttering up in little pulsing flares and vaporizing just within your gaze." It was a mouthful, but Aunt Rose had a way with words. I've already told you about her facility with languages. When Carlos tried it again, Aunt Rose did not take the bait.

I started up the stairs but stopped mid-way in the shadows. Somehow, Carlos had lost track of Sandy Miner's calamities in Montana, and Grandpa, with a magpie's pitch in his voice, had regained his ability to speak between groans.

"Not the whole of the entire truck!" Carlos said, "You'd a' gone out to help, the degree you're fond a' that boy."

"Not me," Aunt Rose said, "I never left the sink or stove after I finished ironing sheets. I just suggested; almost a joke it was. Until he came in battle-scarred and battle-weary, I thought he'd gone over to Saint Pat's to throw the ball with Roger Deans and Todd."

"That boy was sure as hell worth pulling out'a the White River," Grandfather said then paused before, "if you get my drift." You could hardly make him out with his god-awful groaning every other word. "He'll be the one to keep your eye on," he said. "And his way of just letting it be, as if he'd cram a truck with rick wood just as easy and as everyday as you'd cross the street alone!"

When Grandfather said this, I remembered my terror of vehicles charging up and down the streets when we first moved to Chadron. We didn't have that sort of thing up at Fast Horse Creek. And I was glad he'd marked my ability to get to school on my own.

Then Carlos said, "We would not have found the where-with-all to load that truck. Where now, the only thing for us is eat and run. God bless Bear Bait!"

"Amen to that," I heard Aunt Rose chip in then sort of cough and hem a couple times until their conversation stopped. I went back up then with my eyes just focused on the stairs then on the floor. On the counter where I set the pail, I saw twelve spuds all starry-eyed and freshly peeled.

About the Author

R.F. McEwen was born in Chicago, Illinois, in 1945. Since 1962, he has been a professional logger and tree trimmer, working trees throughout the United States as well as in Guyana, South America, during the late 1960s. In 1972, he began teaching Middle School English in Chadron, Nebraska, and has been teaching ever since. He is currently a professor of English at Chadron State College. His work has appeared in numerous journals, including *Kansas Quarterly*, *The Prairie Schooner*, *Melville Extracts* and in *The Yellow Nib*.

CPSIA information can be obtained at www.ICGtesting.com
Printed in the USA
LVOW11s0701170614

390352LV00003B/8/P